There's
No
Such Place As Far Away

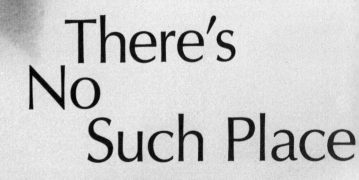

There's
No
Such Place

with paintings by H. Lee Shapiro

Richard Bach

As Far Away

Delta
Trade Paperbacks

A Delta Book
Published by
Dell Publishing
a division of
Bantam Doubleday Dell Publishing Group, Inc.
1540 Broadway
New York, New York 10036

ISBN: 0-385-31927-4

Reprinted by arrangement with Delacorte Press

Manufactured in the United States of America
Published simultaneously in Canada

February 1998

10 9 8 7 6 5 4 3 2 1

KPH

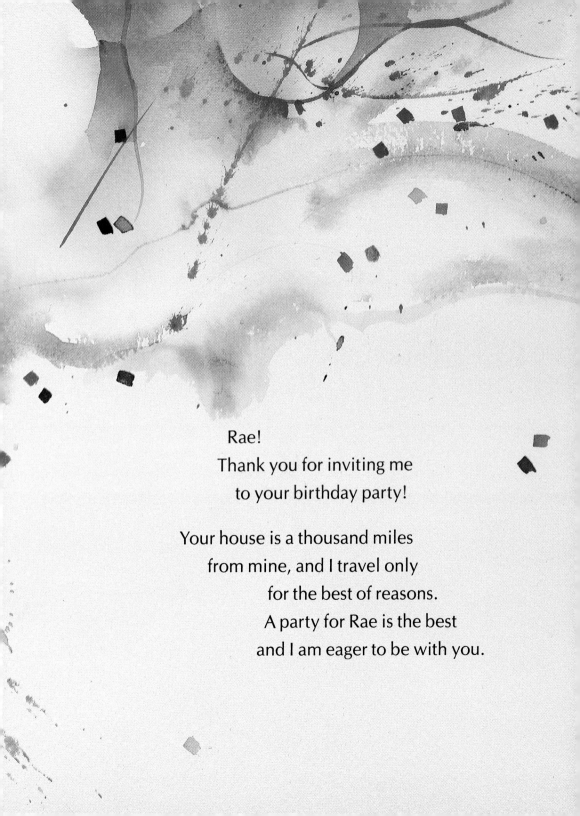

Rae!
Thank you for inviting me
to your birthday party!

Your house is a thousand miles
from mine, and I travel only
for the best of reasons.
A party for Rae is the best
and I am eager to be with you.

I began my journey in the heart of the hummingbird
you and I met long ago. He was friendly as ever,
yet when I told him that little Rae was growing up
and that I was going to her birthday party
with a present, he was puzzled.

We flew for a long while
in silence and at last he said,
"I understand very little
of what you say,
but least of all do I understand
that you are *going* to the party."

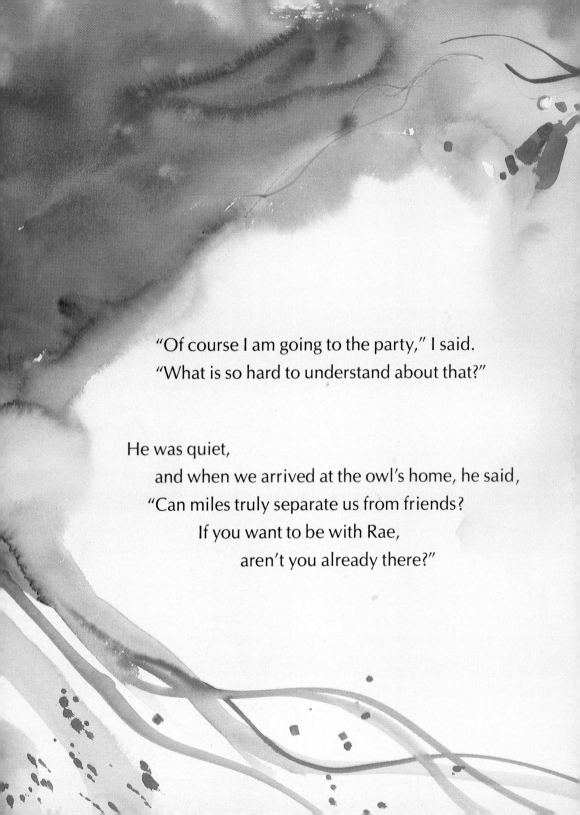

"Of course I am going to the party," I said.
"What is so hard to understand about that?"

He was quiet,
    and when we arrived at the owl's home, he said,
"Can miles truly separate us from friends?
    If you want to be with Rae,
        aren't you already there?"

"Little Rae is growing up
and I am going to her birthday party
with a present," I said to the owl.
It felt strange to say *going* like that,
after talking to Hummingbird, but I said it
that way so Owl would understand.

He, too, flew in silence for a long time.

It was a friendly silence,

but as he delivered me safely to the
home of the eagle, he said, "I understand
very little of what you say, but least
of all do I understand that you
call your friend *little*."

"Of course she is little," I said,
   "because she is not grown up.
      What is so hard
      to understand
      about that?"

                  Owl looked at me
                     with his deep amber eyes,
                  smiled and said,
                  "Think about that."

"Little Rae is growing up and I am going
to her birthday party with a present,"
I said to Eagle. It felt strange now
to say *going* and *little*
after talking with
Hummingbird and Owl,

but I said it that way
so Eagle would understand.

and soared the mountain winds.

out over the mountains,

We flew together

At last she said, "I understand very little of what you say, but least of all do I understand this word *birthday*."

"Of course birthday," I said.
    "We are going to celebrate the hour
    that Rae began, and before which she was not.
        What is so hard to understand about that?"

Eagle curved her wings
into steep dive-flaps
and stepped to a smooth
landing on the desert sand.
"A time before Rae's life
began? Don't you think rather
that it is Rae's life that began
before time ever was?"

"Little Rae is growing up and I am going
to her birthday party with a present,"
I said to Hawk. It felt strange
to say *going* and *little* and *birthday*
after talking with Hummingbird
and Owl and Eagle, but

I said it that way so Hawk
  would understand.

The desert poured by far below us
  and at last she said,
    "You know, I understand very little
      of what you say, but least of all
      do I understand *growing up*."

"Of course growing up," I said.
"Rae is closer to being an adult,
   one more year away from being a child.

   What is so hard to understand about that?"

Hawk landed at last upon a lonely beach.

"One more year from being a child?

and was gone.

And she lifted into the air

That does not sound like growing!"

Seagull, I knew, was very wise. As I flew with him
I thought very carefully and chose words so that
when I spoke he would know I had been learning.

"Seagull," I said at last,
        "why do you fly me to see Rae
            when you know in truth
            I am already with her?"

Seagull turned down
over the sea,
over the hills,
over the streets,
and landed gently
upon your rooftop.

"Because the important thing," he said,
"is for you to know the truth.
Until you know it, until you truly
understand it, you can show it
only in smaller ways, and with
outside help, from machines
and people
and birds.
But remember," he said,
"that not being known
doesn't stop the truth
from being true."

And he was gone.

Now it's time
to open your present.
Gifts of tin and glass
wear out in a day
and are gone.
But I have a better gift for you.

It is a ring for you to wear.
  It sparkles with a special light and
  cannot be taken away by anyone;
  it cannot be destroyed.
  You are the only one in all the world
  who can see the ring that I give you
today, as I was the only one who could
see it when it was mine.

Your ring gives you new power.
Wearing it, you can lift yourself
into the wings of all the birds that fly.

You can see through their golden eyes,
you can touch the wind that sweeps
through their velvet feathers,
you can know the joy of going way up
high above the world and all its cares.
You can stay as long as you want
in the sky,
past the night,
through sunrise,
and when you feel like coming down again,
your questions will have answers and
your worries will have gone.

As anything that cannot be
touched with the hand
or seen with the eye,

your gift grows more
powerful as you use it.

At first
you might use it only when you are outdoors,
watching the birds with whom you fly.

But later on, if you use it well,
it will work with birds
you cannot see,
and last of all you will find
that you'll need
neither ring nor bird
to fly alone above
the quiet of the clouds.

And when that day comes,
 you must give your gift
  to someone you know who will
   use it well, who can learn that
    the only things that matter are those made
    of truth and joy, and not of tin and glass.

Rae, this is the last day-a-year,
special-time celebration that I shall
be with you, learning what I have learned
from our friends the birds.

I cannot go to be with you
   because I am already there.

   You are not little because you are
   already grown, playing among your
   lifetimes as do we all, for
the fun of living.

You have no birthday
because you have always lived;
you were never born, and never will you die.
You are not the child of the people
you call mother and father, but
their fellow-adventurer on a
bright journey to understand
the things that are.

Every gift from a friend
    is a wish for your happiness,
    and so it is with this ring.

Fly free and happy beyond
birthdays and across forever,
and we'll meet now and then
when we wish,
in the midst of the one celebration
that never can end.